A Christmas Carol

by Charles Ludlam

Adapted from the novel by
Charles Dickens

A SAMUEL FRENCH ACTING EDITION

SAMUEL
FRENCH

FOUNDED 1830

NEW YORK HOLLYWOOD LONDON TORONTO

SAMUELFRENCH.COM

Copyright © 1989 by the Estate of Charles Ludlam

ALL RIGHTS RESERVED

CAUTION: Professionals and amateurs are hereby warned that *A CHRISTMAS CAROL* is subject to a Licensing Fee. It is fully protected under the copyright laws of the United States of America, the British Commonwealth, including Canada, and all other countries of the Copyright Union. All rights, including professional, amateur, motion picture, recitation, lecturing, public reading, radio broadcasting, television and the rights of translation into foreign languages are strictly reserved. In its present form the play is dedicated to the reading public only.

The amateur live stage performance rights to *A CHRISTMAS CAROL* are controlled exclusively by Samuel French, Inc., and licensing arrangements and performance licenses must be secured well in advance of presentation. PLEASE NOTE that amateur Licensing Fees are set upon application in accordance with your producing circumstances. When applying for a licensing quotation and a performance license please give us the number of performances intended, dates of production, your seating capacity and admission fee. Licensing Fees are payable one week before the opening performance of the play to Samuel French, Inc., at 45 W. 25th Street, New York, NY 10010.

Licensing Fee of the required amount must be paid whether the play is presented for charity or gain and whether or not admission is charged.

Stock licensing fees quoted upon application to Samuel French, Inc.

For all other rights than those stipulated above, apply to: Fitelson, Lasky, Aslan & Couture, 551 Fifth Avenue, New York, NY 10176, (212) 586-4700; attn: Jerold Couture.

Particular emphasis is laid on the question of amateur or professional readings, permission and terms for which must be secured in writing from Samuel French, Inc.

Copying from this book in whole or in part is strictly forbidden by law, and the right of performance is not transferable.

Whenever the play is produced the following notice must appear on all programs, printing and advertising for the play: "Produced by special arrangement with Samuel French, Inc."

Due authorship credit must be given on all programs, printing and advertising for the play.

ISBN 978-0-573-69865-1   Printed in U.S.A.   #5244

No one shall commit or authorize any act or omission by which the copyright of, or the right to copyright, this play may be impaired.

No one shall make any changes in this play for the purpose of production.

Publication of this play does not imply availability for performance. Both amateurs and professionals considering a production are strongly advised in their own interests to apply to Samuel French, Inc., for written permission before starting rehearsals, advertising, or booking a theatre.

No part of this book may be reproduced, stored in a retrieval system, or transmitted in any form, by any means, now known or yet to be invented, including mechanical, electronic, photocopying, recording, videotaping, or otherwise, without the prior written permission of the publisher.

MUSIC USE NOTE

Licensees are solely responsible for obtaining formal written permission from copyright owners to use copyrighted music in the performance of this play and are strongly cautioned to do so. If no such permission is obtained by the licensee, then the licensee must use only original music that the licensee owns and controls. Licensees are solely responsible and liable for all music clearances and shall indemnify the copyright owners of the play and their licensing agent, Samuel French, Inc., against any costs, expenses, losses and liabilities arising from the use of music by licensees.

IMPORTANT BILLING AND CREDIT REQUIREMENTS

All producers of *A CHRISTMAS CAROL* *must* give credit to the Author of the Play in all programs distributed in connection with performances of the Play, and in all instances in which the title of the Play appears for the purposes of advertising, publicizing or otherwise exploiting the Play and/or a production. The name of the Author *must* appear on a separate line on which no other name appears, immediately following the title and *must* appear in size of type not less than fifty percent of the size of the title type.

A CHRISTMAS CAROL was first produced by the Ridiculous Theatrical Company at the Charles Ludlam Theatre in the December of 1979. The performance was directed by Charles Ludlam, with sets by Bobjack Callejo, and costumes by Gabriel Berry. The main cast was as follows:

EBENEZER SCROOGE . . . . .Charles Ludlam

BOB CRATCHIT . . . . .Bill Vehr

MARLEY'S GHOST . . . . Everett Quinton

CHRISTMAS PAST . . . . Lola Pashalinski

CHRISTMAS PRESENT . . . . .John D. Brockmeyer

TINY TIM . . . . .Renée Pearl

CHARACTERS

SCROOGE

BOB CRATCHIT

NEPHEW

GENTLEMAN #1

GENTLEMAN #2

BOY

MARLEY

CHRISTMAS PAST

LITTLE SCROOGE

FAN

FEZZIWIG

MRS FEZZIWIG

DICK

GUESTS AT THE FEZZIWIGS'

(dancers)

GIRL

SCROOGE-THE-MAN

MOTHER (Girl married)

FATHER

CHRISTMAS PRESENT

MRS CRATCHIT

MISS BELINDA

LITTLE BOY

LITTLE GIRL

MARTHA

TINY TIM

MINERS

NIECE

TOPPER

PLUMP BEAUTY

WANT

IGNORANCE

CHRISTMAS FUTURE

BUSINESSMAN #1

BUSINESSMAN #2

BUSINESSMAN #3

MAN A

MAN B

BAG LADY

OLD JOE

MRS DILBER

HE

SHE

PETER

BOY

Scene One
Scrooge and Marley's Christmas Eve

(SCROOGE counting money. CRATCHIT working on books, shivering with cold. CRATCHIT rises from his work and, looking at the pitiful little fire in his cell, picks up the coal scuttle and attempts to tiptoe past SCROOGE to the coal box.)

SCROOGE. *(speaking without looking up, a habit which gives the distinct impression of his having eyes in the back of his head)* If you waste my coal I shall have to ask you to seek employment elsewhere.

CRATCHIT. But, Mr. Scrooge, it's cold and my fire has nearly gone out.

SCROOGE. Warm yourself at the candle.

(CRATCHIT puts on a muffler and attempts to warm his hands at his candle. Enter Scrooge's NEPHEW.)

NEPHEW. *(cheerily)* Merry Christmas, Uncle! God save you!

SCROOGE. Bah! Humbug!

NEPHEW. Christmas a humbug, Uncle! You don't mean that, I am sure.

SCROOGE. I do. Merry Christmas! What right have you to be merry? What reason have you to be merry? You're poor enough.

NEPHEW. Come then, what right have you to be dismal? What reason have you to be morose? You're rich enough.

SCROOGE. *(after a brief reflection pause in which he fails to come up with a better rejoinder)* Bah! Humbug!

NEPHEW. Don't be cross, Uncle.

SCROOGE. What else can I be when I live in such a world of fools as this? Merry Christmas! Out upon Merry Christmas! What's Christmastime to you but a time for paying bills without money, a time for finding yourself a year older, and not an hour richer, a time for balancing your books and having every item in 'em through a round dozen of months presented dead against you? If I could work my will, every idiot who goes about with "Merry Christmas" on his lips, should be boiled with his own pudding and burled with a stake of holly through his heart. He should!

NEPHEW. Uncle!

SCROOGE. Nephew! Keep Christmas in your own way and let me keep it in mine.

NEPHEW Keep it! But you don't keep it.

SCROOGE. Let me leave it alone, then. Much good it may do you! Much good it has ever done you!

NEPHEW. There are many things from which I might have derived good, by which I have not profited, I dare say, Christmas among the rest. But I am sure I have always thought of Christmastime, from when it has come round – apart from the veneration due to its sacred name and origin, if anything belonging to it can be apart from that – as a good time. A kind, forgiving, charitable, pleasant time, the only time I know of, in the long calendar of the year, when men and women seem by one consent to open their shut-up hearts freely, and to think of people below them as if they really were fellow passengers to the grave, and not another race of creatures bound on other journeys. And therefore, Uncle, though it has never put a scrap of gold or silver in my pocket, I believe that it *has* done me good, and *will* do me good, and I say, God bless it!

(**CRATCHIT** *momentarily applauds and, upon catching himself, pokes the fire, extinguishing the last coal.*)

SCROOGE. *(to* **CRATCHIT***)* Let me hear another sound from *you* and you'll keep your Christmas by losing your situation. *(to his* **NEPHEW***)* You're quite a powerful speaker, sir. I wonder you don't go into Parliament.

NEPHEW.' Don't be angry, Uncle. Come! Dine with us to-morrow.

SCROOGE. I'll see you hanged first.

NEPHEW. *(crying out)* But why? Why?

SCROOGE. Why did you get married?

NEPHEW. Because I fell in love.

SCROOGE. *(mockingly)* Because you fell in love! Good Afternoon!

NEPHEW. Nay, Uncle, but you never came to see me before that happened. Why give it as a reason for not coming now?

SCROOGE. Good afternoon.

NEPHEW. I want nothing from you, I ask nothing of you, why cannot we be friends?

SCROOGE. Good afternoon.

NEPHEW. I am sorry, with all my heart, to find you so resolute. We have never had any quarrel to which I have been a party. But I have made the trial in homage to Christmas, and I'll keep my Christmas humor to the last. So, a merry Christmas, Uncle!

SCROOGE. Good afternoon!

NEPHEW. And a happy New Year!

SCROOGE. Good afternoon.

NEPHEW. *(to* **CRATCHIT** *in the anteroom as he leaves)* And a very merry Christmas to you.

CRATCHIT. *(warmly)* Merry Christmas, Fred.

SCROOGE. *(muttering)* There's another fellow, my clerk, with fifteen shillings a week, and a wife and family, talking about a merry Christmas. I'll retire to Bedlam.

(**CRATCHIT** *lets Scrooge's* **NEPHEW** *out and two other* **GENTLEMEN** *in.)*

FIRST GENTLEMAN. Scrooge and Marley's I believe. Have I the pleasure of addressing Mr. Scrooge or Mr. Marley?

SCROOGE. Mr. Marley has been dead these seven years. He died seven years ago this very night.

FIRST GENTLEMAN. We have no doubt his liberality is well represented by his surviving partner.

(Presents his credentials. At the ominous word "liberality" SCROOGE *frowns, shakes his head, and hands his credentials back.)*

At this festive season of the year, Mr. Scrooge, it is more than usually desirable that we should make some slight provision for the poor and destitute, who suffer greatly at the present time. Many thousands are in want of common necessaries, hundreds of thousands are in want of common comforts, sir.

SCROOGE. Are there no prisons?

FIRST GENTLEMAN. Plenty of prisons.

SCROOGE.' And the union workhouses? Are they still in operation?

FIRST GENTLEMAN. They are. I wish I could say they were not.

SCROOGE. The treadmill and the poor law are in full vigor, then?

FIRST GENTLEMAN. Both very busy, sir.

SCROOGE. Good I was afraid, from what you said at first, that something had occurred to stop them in their useful course. I'm very glad to hear it.

FIRST GENTLEMAN. Under the impression that they scarcely furnish Christian cheer of mind or body to the multitude, a few of us are endeavoring to raise a fund to buy the Poor some meat and drink, and means of warmth. We choose this time, because it is a time, of all others, when Want is keenly felt, and abundance rejoices. What shall I put you down for?

SCROOGE. Nothing.

FIRST GENTLEMAN. You wish to remain anonymous?

SCROOGE. I wish to be left alone. Since you ask me what I wish, Gentlemen, that is my answer. I don't make merry myself at Christmas, and I can't afford to make idle people merry. I help to support the establishments

I have mentioned – they cost enough – and those who are badly off must go there.

FIRST GENTLEMAN. Many can't go there and many would rather die.

SCROOGE. If they would rather die, they had better do it, and decrease the surplus population. Besides – excuse me – I don't know that.

FIRST GENTLEMAN. But you might know it.

SCROOGE. It's not my business. It's enough for a man to understand his own business, and not to interfere with other people's. Mine occupies me constantly. Good afternoon, gentlemen!

(*The* GENTLEMEN *exist.* SCROOGE *resumes his work with a chuckle. Fog obscures the clock in the church tower usually visible from Scrooge's Gothic window. Voices of carolers in the street below.* BOY *at keyhole sings, "God rest ye merry gentlemen, let nothing you dismay."* SCROOGE *throws a ruler at him. Rising with ill-will and crossing to the window*)

Quiet down there! Quiet, imbeciles! How's a man to work with that racket'?

CRATCHIT. It's closing time anyway, Mr. Scrooge.

SCROOGE. So it is. You'll want all day tomorrow, I suppose?

CRATCHIT. If quite convenient, sir.

SCROOGE. It's not convenient, and it's not fair. If I was to dock you half a crown for it, you'd think yourself ill-used, I'll be bound? And yet you don't think *me* ill-used when I pay a day's wages for no work.

CRATCHIT. (*smiling faintly*) It's only once a year, sir.

SCROOGE. A poor excuse for picking a man's pocket every twenty-fifth of December! (*buttons up his greatcoat to the chin*) But I suppose you must have the whole day. Be here all the earlier next morning!

CRATCHIT. I will, Mr. Scrooge.

SCROOGE. (*growls and exits*)

Scene Two
Scrooge's Apartment

(SCROOGE and the lighted candle are all that is visible on the stage. SCROOGE sits him down by a meager fire and slurps a bowl of gruel. There is the sound of the howling of the wind, which produces the effect of ghostly voices. SCROOGE goes about the room to see if everything is all right.)

SCROOGE. *(talking to himself)* Nobody under the table. Nobody under the sofa. Nobody under the bed. Nobody in the closet. Nobody in my dressing gown – except me. Lumber room as usual. Old fireguard, old shoes, two fish baskets, washingstand, poker. Everything is as it should be.

(goes and double locks the door, then sits down and begins to slurp his gruel again)

Humbug!

(Suddenly a bell hanging by the wall begins to swing by itself and then to ring. SCROOGE stares at this phenomenon in horror. [SCROOGE sees in the door's knocker Marley's face.] The sound of footsteps and dragging chains can be heard, at first far off, but then they come nearer and nearer.)

Ghosts? It's humbug still! I won't believe it.

(MARLEY'S GHOST enters, dragging chains made of cashboxes, keys, padlocks, ledgers, deeds, and heavy purses wrought in steel. The dying flame in the fireplace leaps up and dies down again. Cold and caustic.)

How now! What do you want with me?

MARLEY. Much.

SCROOGE. Who are you?

MARLEY. Ask me who I *was*.

SCROOGE. *(raising his voice)* Who *were* you, then? You're particular – for a shade.

MARLEY. In life I was your partner, Jacob Marley.

SCROOGE. Can you can you sit down?

MARLEY. I can.

SCROOGE. Do it, then.

MARLEY. *(taking a seat on the opposite side of the fireplace as though he were quite used to it)* You don't believe in me.

SCROOGE. I don't.

MARLEY. What evidence would you have of my reality beyond that of your senses?

SCROOGE. I don't know.

MARLEY. Why do you doubt your senses?

SCROOGE. Because, a little thing affects them. A slight disorder of the stomach makes them cheats. You may be an undigested bit of beef, a blot of mustard, a crumb of cheese, a fragment of an underdone potato. There's more of gravy than of grave about you, whatever you are.

(Laughs feebly at his own joke. The ghost however is not amused.)

You see this toothpick?

MARLEY. I do.

SCROOGE. You are not looking at it.

MARLEY. But I see it notwithstanding.

SCROOGE. Well! I have but to swallow this, and be for the rest of my days persecuted by a legion of goblins, all of my own creation. Humbug, I tell you – humbug!

MARLEY. *(Lets out a frightful cry and shakes its chains. Then removes its own arm and shakes the gory end of it threateningly at* **SCROOGE.***)*

SCROOGE. *(falling on his knees and clasping his hands before his face)* Mercy! Dreadful apparition, why do you trouble me?

MARLEY. Man of the worldly mind! Do you believe in me or not?

SCROOGE. I do. I must. But why do spirits walk the earth and why do they come to me?

MARLEY. It is required of every man that the spirit within him should walk abroad among his fellowmen, and travel far and wide, and if that spirit goes not forth in life, it is condemned to do so after death. It is doomed to wander through the world – oh, woe is me! – and witness what it cannot share, but might have shared on earth, and turned to happiness! *(Cries out and shakes its chains and wrings its shadowy hands.)*

SCROOGE. *(trembling)* You are fettered. Tell me why?

MARLEY. I wear the chain I forged in life. I made it link by link, and yard by yard, I girded it on of my own free will, and of my own free will I wore it. Is its pattern strange to *you*? Or do you know the weight and length of the strong coil you bear yourself? It was full as heavy and as long as this, seven Christmas Eves ago. You have labored on it since. It is a ponderous chain!

SCROOGE. *(trembling more and more, looks about him for the chain but see nothing)* Jacob, old Jacob Marley, tell me more. Speak comfort to me, Jacob.

MARLEY. I have none to give. It comes from other regions, Ebenezer Scrooge, and is conveyed by other ministers, to other kinds of men. Nor can I tell you all I would. A very little more is all permitted to me. I cannot rest, I cannot stay! I cannot linger anywhere. My spirit never walked beyond our counting-house – mark me! – in life my spirit never roved beyond the narrow limits of our money-changing hole, and weary journeys lie before me!

SCROOGE. *(putting his hands in his pockets thoughtfully)* You must have been very slow about it, Jacob.

MARLEY. Slow?

SCROOGE. Seven years dead and traveling all the time?

MARLEY. The whole time, no rest, no peace. Incessant torture of remorse.

SCROOGE. You travel fast?

MARLEY. On the wings of the wind.

SCROOGE. You might have got over a great quantity of ground in seven years.

MARLEY. *(crying out again and clanking its chains hideously)* Oh! Captive bound and double-ironed, not to know that ages of incessant labor, by immortal creatures, for this earth, must pass into eternity before the good of which it is susceptible is all developed. Not to know that any Christian spirit working kindly in its little sphere, whatever it may be, will find its mortal life too short for its vast means of usefulness. Not to know that no space of regret can make amends for one life's opportunities misused! Yet such was I! Oh! Such was I!

SCROOGE. But you were always a good man of business, Jacob.

MARLEY. *(crying out and wringing his hands again)* Business! Mankind was my business. The common welfare was my business, charity, mercy, forbearance, and benevolence, were all my business! The dealings of my trade were but a drop of water in the comprehensive ocean of my business! *(holds up its chain and flings it on the ground again)* At this tune of the rolling year, I suffer most. Why did I walk through crowds of fellow beings with my eyes turned down, and never raise them to that blessed Star which led the Wise Men to a poor abode? Were there no poor homes to which its light would have conducted *me*? Hear me! My time is nearly gone.

SCROOGE. I will, but don't be hard upon me! Don't be flowery, Jacob! Pray!

MARLEY. How it is that I appear before you in a shape that you can see, I may not tell. I have sat invisible beside you many and many a day

*(**SCROOGE** shivers and wipes the perspiration from his brow.)*

That is no light part of my penance. I am here tonight to warn you that you have yet a chance and hope of escaping my fate. A chance and hope of my procuring, Ebenezer.

SCROOGE. You were always a good friend to me. Thank'ee!

MARLEY. You will be haunted by Three Spirits.

SCROOGE. *(his face falling and in a faltering tone)* Is that the chance and hope you mentioned, Jacob?

MARLEY. It is.

SCROOGE. I...I think I'd rather not.

MARLEY. Without their visits you cannot hope to shun the path I tread. Expect the first tomorrow when the bell tolls one.

SCROOGE. Couldn't I take 'em all at once and have it over, Jacob?

MARLEY. Expect the second when the bell tolls two. And the third when the last stroke of three has ceased to vibrate. Look to see me no more, and look that, for your own sake, you remember what has passed between us.

(rises and walks backward toward the window, which opens by itself, and passes out into the foggy night air amid the ghostly sounds of lamentation)

Good night, Ebenezer. I must join the others, they have come for me. Hear them? Our misery is this: we wish to interfere, for good, in human matters, but have lost the power forever. Ah! there's a wretched woman with an infant huddled in a doorway...

(fades into mist amid a mournful spirit dirge)

SCROOGE. *(goes to the door)* The door locked! Hum –

*(The word is choked off by emotion and **SCROOGE** falls into bed and asleep, fatigued by the labors of the day, his glimpse of the Invisible World, the dull conversation of the Ghost and the lateness of the hour.)*

Scene Three
Scrooge in Bed

(The bell in the neighboring church chimes and **SCROOGE** *awakes and listens to it. The bell chimes twelve times.)*

SCROOGE. Why, it isn't possible that I can have slept through a whole day and far into another night. It isn't possible that anything has happened to the sun, and this is twelve at noon. *(He goes to the window and looks out.)* Still nighttime. Hmmm. *(He gets back into bed.)* Marley's ghost. Was it a dream or not? Marley warned me of a visitation when the bell tolls one. Well, I can no more go to sleep now than go to heaven. I may as well lie awake until that blasted hour has passed.

(He tosses and turns uncomfortably, plumps his pillow, tries to arrange the covers, when at length the sound of the bell breaks upon his listening ear. Ding, dong!)

A quarter past. *(Ding, dong!)* Half past! *(Ding, dong!)* A quarter to it! *(Ding, dong!)* The hour itself, and nothing else!

(The bell tolls one. There is a flash of light. **SCROOGE** *draws the curtains of his bed hides his head under the bedclothes. The curtains reopen by an unseen hand revealing him in this ludicrous posture. At this moment the* **SPIRIT OF CHRISTMAS PAST** *appears. It is a child with long gray hair crowned with a ring of lighted candles. Both old and young at once like the different times of our lives as perceived through memory it carries a wand of fresh green holly and its white tunic is trimmed with summer flowers.)*

Are you the Spirit, sir, whose coming was foretold to me?

CHRISTMAS PAST. *(gently)* I am!

SCROOGE. Who and what are you?

CHRISTMAS PAST. I am the Ghost of Christmas Past.

SCROOGE. Long past?

CHRISTMAS PAST. No. Your past.

SCROOGE. You'd better put out those candles on your head before they burn too low.

CHRISTMAS PAST. What! Would you so soon with worldly hands put out the light I give? Is it not enough that you are one of those whose passions dimmed my light, in hopes that I would through whole trains of years in darkness lose my way?

SCROOGE. No offense meant. But what business brings you here?

CHRISTMAS PAST. Your welfare!

SCROOGE. Much obliged! *(then aside)* Although a good night's sleep would have done me more good!

CHRISTMAS PAST. Your reclamation, then. Take heed! *(putting out its strong hand and clasping him by the arm)* Rise! and walk with me! *(leads him to the window)*

SCROOGE. *(clasping the Spirit's robes in supplication)* Please, I am a mortal and liable to fall!

CHRISTMAS PAST. Bear but a touch of my hand *there (lays its hand upon his heart),* and you shall be upheld in more than this!

(They pass through the window and as they do, the walls of the room disappear, and they find themselves on a country road on a clear winter's day. There is snow upon the ground.)

SCROOGE. *(clasping his hands together)* Good heaven! I was bred in this place. I was a boy here! There are a thousand odors floating in the air, and each brings back a thousand thoughts and joys and hopes and cares long, long forgotten!

CHRISTMAS PAST. Your lip is trembling, and what is that upon your cheek?

SCROOGE. *(with a catch in his tone)* It's just a pimple. Lead on. Lead me where you will.

CHRISTMAS PAST. You recollect the way?

SCROOGE. Recollect it? I could walk it blindfolded.

CHRISTMAS PAST. Strange to have forgotten it for so many years. Let us go on.

*(They walk down the road, **SCROOGE** recognizing every gate, post, and tree. Boys on ponies pass, full of laughter, shouting to each other as they pass. **SCROOGE** knows and names every one of them. The walls are scrim, the images cinema.)*

SCROOGE. Why there are all the boys from St James's. And there's Dan Ireland and Toady! Dear old Toady!

CHRISTMAS PAST. Toady?

SCROOGE. The pony is Toady. Dan got him for Christmas. Ha ha! Hey Dan! Dan!

CHRISTMAS PAST. These are but shadows of things that have been. They have no consciousness of us. The school is not quite deserted. A solitary child, neglected by his friends, is left there still.

SCROOGE. I know it. *(sobs)* It's my poor forgotten self as I used to be. *(sits down and weeps)*

*(There is the image of a boy reading by candlelight in an atmosphere of not enough to eat. The spirit touches **SCROOGE** gently upon the arm and points to the image of the boy, next to which the figure of a man has appeared.)*

CHRISTMAS PAST. Look.

SCROOGE. *(in ecstasy)* Why, it's Ali Baba! It's dear old honest Ali Baba! Yes, yes, I know! One Christmastime when yonder solitary child was left alone he *did* come for the first time, just like that. Poor boy! And Valentine and his wild brother, Orson, there they go! And what's-his-name, who was put down in his drawers, asleep, at the Gate of Damascus, don't you see him! And the Sultan's Groom turned upside down by the Genii, there he is upon his head! Serves him right I'm glad of it. What business had *he* to be married to the princess?

*(**SCROOGE** is in a heightened state somewhere between laughing and crying.)*

SCROOGE. *(cont.)* There's the parrot! Green body and yellow tail, with a thing like a lettuce growing out of the top of his head, there he is! Poor Robinson Crusoe, he called him, when he came home again after sailing around the island. Poor Robinson Crusoe, where have you been, Robinson Crusoe? The man thought he was dreaming, but he wasn't. It was the parrot, you know. There goes Friday, running for his life to the little creek! Halloa! Hoop! Halloo! *(with a rapidity of transition very foreign to his usual character)* Poor boy! *(cries again)* I wish *(puts his hand in his pocket after drying his eyes on his cuff)* but it's too late now.

CHRISTMAS PAST. What is the matter?

SCROOGE. Nothing. Nothing. There was a boy singing a Christmas carol at my door last night. I should like to have given him something, that's all.

CHRISTMAS PAST *(smiles thoughtfully and waves its hand)* Let us see another Christmas!

(The cinematic image dissolves. The boy is older now. The room in which he sits is more run-down. The door opens and a **LITTLE GIRL** *younger than the boy enters and throws her arms around the little boy and kisses him.)*

FAN. Dear, dear brother. *(kisses him again)* I have come to bring you home, dear brother! *(claps her tiny hands and bends down to laugh)* To bring you home, home, home!

LITTLE SCROOGE. Home, little Fan?

FAN. *(brimful of glee)* Yes! Home for good and all. Home for ever and ever. Father is so much kinder than he used to be that home's like heaven! He spoke so gently to me one dear night when I was going to bed, that I was not afraid to ask him once more if you might come home, and he said, Yes, you should, and sent me in a coach to bring you. And you're to be a man! And are never to come back here, but first, we're to be together all the Christmas long, and have the merriest time in all the world.

LITTLE SCROOGE. You are quite a woman, little Fan!

(The little girl laughs and claps her hands and drags him in her childish eagerness toward the door.)

VOICE OF GRUFF SCHOOLMASTER. *(off)* Bring down master Scrooge's box there! He's going home.

FAN. *(to the little boy, gleefully)* Did you hear that, Ebenezer? Home! Home! *(laughs childishly for joy)* Home! *(Her voice fades away.)*

CHRISTMAS PAST. Always a delicate creature whom a breath might have withered. But she had a large heart!

SCROOGE. So she had. You're right. I'll not gainsay it, Spirit, God forbid!

CHRISTMAS PAST. She died a woman and had, as I think, children.

SCROOGE. One child.

CHRISTMAS PAST. True. Your nephew!

SCROOGE. *(uneasily)* Yes.

CHRISTMAS PAST. *(pointing to a door in a city street scene)* Do you know this warehouse door?

SCROOGE. Know it! Was I apprenticed here?

(They go in. There they see an old gentleman at a desk so high he almost hits his head on the ceiling.)

Why, it's old Fezziwig! Bless his heart, it's Fezziwig alive again!

FEZZIWLG. *(laying down his book and his pen, looking up at the clock, which points to the hour of seven, adjusting his capacious waistcoat, and laughing all over himself from his shoes to his organ of benevolence, calls out in a comfortable, oily, rich, fat, jovial voice)* Yo ho, there! Ebenezer! Dick!

(Scrooge's former self, now grown into a young man, enters with a fellow apprentice.)

SCROOGE. Dick Wilkins to be sure! Bless me, yes. There he is. He was very much attached to me, was Dick. Poor Dick! Dear, dear!

FEZZIWIG. Yo ho, my boys! No more work tonight. Christmas Eve, Dick. Christmas, Ebenezer! Let's have the shutters up! *(claps his hands)* Before a man can say, Jack Robinson!

(The young men charge about it till they are panting like racehorses. Skipping down from his high desk with wonderful agility)

Hilli-ho! Clear away, my lads, and let's have lots of room here! Hilli-ho, Dick! Chirrup, Ebenezer!

(The two young men clear away every movable until the warehouse is a ballroom. In comes a fiddler and begins to play merrily. In comes MRS FEZZIWIG, one vast substantial smile. In come the three MISS FEZZIWIGS, beaming and lovable. In come the six young FOLLOWERS whose hearts they broke. In come the HOUSEMAID, the BAKER, and the MILKMAN. Until the room is all cheer, all laughter, all dancing away or standing in affectionate groupings. Then the fiddler strikes up "Sir Roger de Coverly" and old FEZZIWIG stands out to dance a reel with MRS FEZZIWIG. "Hold hands with your partner, bow and curtsy, thread-the-needle, and back again to your place." Old FEZZIWIG outdances them all, young and old, and comes out without so much as a stagger. The clock strikes eleven and the domestic ball breaks up. Then MR and MRS FEZZIWIG take their places at either side of the door and, smiling, shake hands with each and every guest and bid them good night and merry Christmas. All thank them profusely.)

CHRISTMAS PAST. A small matter to make these silly folks so full of gratitude.

SCROOGE. Small!

CHRISTMAS PAST. Why! Is it not? He has spent but a few pounds of your mortal money. Three or four, perhaps. Is that so much that he deserves this praise?

SCROOGE. It isn't that. *(heatedly)* Isn't that, Spirit. He has the power to render us happy or unhappy, to make our service light or burdensome, a pleasure or a toil. Say that his power lies in words and looks, in things so slight and insignificant that it is impossible to add and count 'em up, what then? The happiness he gives is quite as great as if it cost a fortune. *(feels the spirit's glance and stops)*

CHRISTMAS PAST. What is the matter?

SCROOGE. Nothing particular.

CHRISTMAS PAST. Something, I think?

SCROOGE. No, no. I should like to be able to say a word or two to my clerk just now! That's all.

CHRISTMAS PAST. My time grows short. Quick!

(A somewhat older and greedier SCROOGE appears before them. Beside him sits a GIRL in mourning dress with tears sparkling in her eyes.)

GIRL. *(softly)* It matters little. To you very little. Another idol has displaced me, and if it can cheer and comfort you in time to come, as I would have tried to do, I have no just cause to grieve.

SCROOGE-THE-MAN. What idol has displaced you?

GIRL. A golden one.

SCROOGE-THE-MAN. This is the evenhanded dealing of the world! There is nothing on which it is so hard as poverty, and there is nothing which it professes to condemn with such severity as the pursuit of wealth!

GIRL. *(gently)* You fear the world too much. All your other hopes have merged into the hope of being beyond the chance of its sordid reproach. I have seen your nobler aspirations fall off one by one, until the master passion, Gain, engrosses you. Have I not?

SCROOGE-THE-MAN. What then? Even if I have grown so much wiser, what then? I am not changed towards you. Am I?

GIRL. *(shaking her head)* Our contract is an old one. It was made when we mere both poor and content to be so, until, in good season, we should improve our worldly fortune by our patient industry. You *are* changed. When it was made you were another man.

SCROOGE-THE-MAN. *(impatiently)* I was a boy.

GIRL. Your own feeling tells you that you were nor what you are. I am. That which promised happiness when we were one in heart, is fraught with misery now that we are two. How often and how keenly I have thought of this, I will not say. It is enough that I *have* thought of it, and can release you.

SCROOGE-THE-MAN. Have I ever sought release?

GIRL. In words, no. Never.

SCROOGE-THE-MAN. In what, then?

GIRL. In a changed nature, in an altered spirit, in another atmosphere of life, another hope as its great end. In everything that ever made my love of any worth or value in your sight. If this had never been between us *(looking mildly but steadily upon him)*, tell me, would you seek me out and try to win me now? Ah, no!

SCROOGE-THE-MAN. *(almost yielding to the supposition in spite of himself)* So you think not?

GIRL. I would gladly think otherwise if I could. Heaven knows! When I have learned a Truth like this, I know how strong and irresistible it must be. But if you were free today, tomorrow, yesterday, can even I believe that you would choose a dowerless girl – you who, in your very confidence with her, weigh everything by Gain or, choosing her, if for a moment you were false enough to your one guiding principle to do so, do I not know that your repentance and regret would surely follow? I do, and I release you. With a full heart for the love of him you once were. *(turns from him)* You may – the memory of what is past half makes me hope you will – have pain in this. A very, very brief time, and you will dismiss the recollection of it, gladly, as an unprofitable dream, from which it happened well that you awoke. May you be happy in the life you have chosen! *(She leaves him.)*

SCROOGE. Spirit! Show me no more! Why do you delight to torture me?

CHRISTMAS PAST. One shadow more!

SCROOGE. *(crying out)* No more! No more! I don't wish to see it. Show me no more!

(SCROOGE tries to turn away but the SPIRIT pinions him with its arms and forces him to look. A domestic scene appears with the girl now turned into a beautiful matron surrounded by children playing noisily. The FATHER enters laden with Christmas presents. They sit by their fire surrounded by their loving children.)

FATHER. Belle, I saw an old friend of yours this afternoon.

MOTHER. Who was it?

FATHER. Guess.

MOTHER. How can I? Tut, I don't know. *(laughing)* Mr. Scrooge.

FATHER. Mr. Scrooge it was. I passed his office window, and as it was not shut up, and he had a candle inside, I could scarcely help seeing him. His partner lies upon the point of death, I hear, and there he sat alone. Quite alone in the world, I do believe.

SCROOGE. *(in a broken voice)* Spirit, remove me from this place.

CHRISTMAS PAST. I told you these were shadows of the things that have been. That they are what they are, do not blame me!

SCROOGE. Remove me! I cannot bear it! *(looking into the ghost's face)* Your face! I see in your face fragments of all the faces you have shown me! *(wrestling with the ghost)* Leave me! Take me back! Haunt me no longer!

(While SCROOGE struggles desperately the ghost is undisturbed by any of his efforts and shows no visible resistance. In fact his light shines all the brighter until SCROOGE forces an extinguisher cap – a giant candle-snuff – over it, and reeling back to his bed, falls into a heavy sleep.)

Scene Four
The Second of the Three Spirits

(The bell strikes one. **SCROOGE** *with fear and trembling opens the door to an adjoining room wherein he finds a jolly giant, glorious to see, upon a pile of holiday edibles, crowned with holly and mistletoe and carrying a torch like the horn of plenty.)*

CHRISTMAS PRESENT. Come in! Come in, and know me better, man! I am the Ghost of Christmas Present. Look upon me! You have never seen the like of me before!

*(***GHOST OF CHRISTMAS PRESENT*** is a composite of Father Christmas and his forerunners in the Roman Saturnalia cults. He wears a flowering green robe trimmed in white fur out of which bare feet and breast protrude. His dark brown curls are long and free, free as his genial face, his sparkling eye, his open hand, his cheery voice, his unconstrained demeanor, and his joyful air. Girdled round his waist is an antique scabbard with no sword in it whose ancient sheath is eaten up with rust.)*

SCROOGE. Never.

CHRISTMAS PRESENT. Have you never walked forth with the younger members of my family, meaning – for I am very young – my elder brothers born in these later years?

SCROOGE. I don't think I have. I am afraid I have not. Have you had many brothers, Spirit?

CHRISTMAS PRESENT. More than eighteen hundred.

SCROOGE. *(mutters)* A tremendous family to provide for! *(The spirit rises. Submissively)* Spirit, conduct me where you will. I went forth last night on compulsion, and I learnt a lesson which is working now. Tonight, if you have aught to teach me, let me profit by it.

CHRISTMAS PRESENT. Touch my robe!

*(**SCROOGE** does this and at his touch the room once again disappears and he finds himself once again in the street. It is snowing and the merry pageant of going home for Christmas is acted out in pantomime as the populace hurries to their hearths and snowball fights and grocery shopping.)*

SCROOGE. Is there a peculiar flavor in what you sprinkle from your torch?

CHRISTMAS PRESENT. There is. My own.

SCROOGE. Would it apply to any kind of dinner on this day?

CHRISTMAS PRESENT. To any kindly given. To a poor one most.

SCROOGE. Why to a poor one most?

CHRISTMAS PRESENT. Because it needs it most.

SCROOGE. *(after a moment's thought)* Spirit, I wonder you, of all the beings in the many worlds about us, should desire to cramp these people's opportunities of innocent enjoyment.

CHRISTMAS PRESENT. *(shocked)* I?

SCROOGE. You seek to close these places on the Seventh Day? And it comes to the same thing.

CHRISTMAS PRESENT. *I* seek?

SCROOGE. Forgive me if I am wrong. It has been done in your name, or at least in that of your family.

CHRISTMAS PRESENT. There are some upon this earth of yours, who lay claim to know us, and who do their deeds of passion, pride, ill-will, hatred, envy, bigotry, and selfishness in our name, who are as strange to us and all our kith and kin, as if they had never lived. Remember that and charge their doings on themselves, not us.

*(On they trudge to Bob Cratchit's house, where the **SPIRIT** blesses it with his torch.)*

SCROOGE. Whose house is that?

CHRISTMAS PRESENT. Your clerk's.

MRS CRATCHIT. What has ever got your precious father, then? And your brother, Tiny Tim, and Martha wasn't as late last Christmas Day by half an hour!

MISS BELINDA. Here's Martha, Mother!

LITTLE BOY & GIRL. Here's Martha, Mother! Hurrah, there's *such* a goose, Martha!

MRS CRATCHIT. Why bless your heart alive, my dear, here you are! *(kisses her a dozen times and taking off her shawl and bonnet for her with officious zeal)*

MARTHA. We'd a deal of work to finish up last night and had to clear away this morning, Mother.

MRS CRATCHIT. Well! Never mind so long as ye are come. Sit ye down before the fire, my dear, and have a warm, Lord bless ye!

LITTLE BOY & GIRL. No, no! There's father coming. *(running everywhere at once)* Hide, Martha, hide!

*(The three children run and hide. **BOB CRATCHIT** enters, his threadbare clothes darned up and brushed to look seasonable, with **TINY TIM** upon his shoulder. **TINY TIM** carries a little crutch and his body is supported by an iron frame.)*

CRATCHIT. *(looking around)* Why, where's our Martha?

MRS CRATCHIT. Not coming.

CRATCHIT. *(with a sudden declension in his high spirits)* Not coming! Not coming upon Christmas Day!

MARTHA. *(coming out from behind the closet door and throwing herself into his arms)* Don't be disappointed, Father, it's only a joke!

*(The little ones hustle **TINY TIM** off to the washbasin.)*

MRS CRATCHIT. And how did little Tim behave?

CRATCHIT. *(tremulous)* As good as gold and better. Somehow he gets thoughtful sitting by himself so much, and thinks the strangest things you ever heard. He told me, coming home, that he hoped the people saw him in the church because he was a cripple, and it might be pleasant to them to remember upon Christmas

Day, who made lame beggars walk and blind men see. *(His voice trembles more.)* But Tiny Tim is growing strong and hearty.

(Tiny Tim's little crutch can be heard upon the floor as he enters and takes his place upon his stool by the fire. **CRATCHIT** *serves up some punch. They all bustle about preparations for the meal. They set the table, finally settle down. The children bring in the goose.)*

ALL. The goose! The goose! So big! Mmmm, tender. Delicious. What flavor! And so cheap! Pass the potatoes. Pass the applesauce! Pass the gravy!

TINY TIM. *(beating his knife and fork on the table, cries feebly)* Hurrah!

(Long silent sequence while they eat.)

MISS BELINDA. Plates! Your plate, Father. Give me your plate, Tim. Martha, pass me Tim's plate. I'm going to bring in the pudding.

MRS CRATCHIT. *(rising)* I can't watch. I'm too nervous.

CRATCHIT. There there, I'm sure it will be fine.

MRS CRATCHIT. It might not be done enough. I should have left it on longer.

MISS BELINDA. Don't worry, Mother. It's been on a good while.

MRS CRATCHIT. I can't look. Suppose it should break in turning out?

MISS BELINDA. Suppose somebody should have got over the wall of the backyard, and stolen it, while we were making merry with the goose.

LITTLE BOY & GIRL. *(loud)* They'd just better not have! Run and see! Save the pudding. Watch out for the crooks!

(They turn out the pudding and light it.)

CRATCHIT. Oh, a wonderful pudding! This is the best pudding you've made since we were married.

MRS CRATCHIT. Well that's a great weight off my mind. I had my doubts about the quantity of flour.

SCROOGE. Rather a small pudding, isn't it, for so large a family?

CHRISTMAS PRESENT. Shhh! They'd think it heresy to say so. Any Cratchit would blush to hint at such a thing.

CRATCHIT. *(proposing a toast)* A Merry Christmas to us all, my dears. God bless us!

THE FAMILY. God bless us!

TINY TIM. God bless us every one!

(CRATCHIT hugs TINY TIM's frail body and keeps him by his side as if he feared he might be taken from him.)

SCROOGE. *(with a newly awakened interest)* Spirit, tell me if Tiny Tim will live.

CHRISTMAS PRESENT. I see a vacant seat in the poor chimney corner, and a crutch without an owner carefully preserved. If these shadows remain unaltered by the Future, the child will die.

SCROOGE. No, no! Oh no, kind Spirit! Say he will be spared.

CHRISTMAS PRESENT. If these shadows remain unaltered by the Future, none other of my race will find him here. What then? If he be like to die, he had better do it and decrease the surplus population.

*(On hearing his own words, **SCROOGE** hangs his head, overcome with penitence and grief.)*

Man, if man you be in heart, not adamant, forbear that wicked cant until you have discovered What the surplus is, and Where it is. Will you decide what men shall live, what men shall die? It may be, that in the sight of Heaven, you are more unfit to live than millions like this poor man's child. Oh God! To hear the Insect on the leaf pronouncing on the too much life among his hungry brothers in the dust!

*(**SCROOGE** bends before the Ghost's rebuke and, trembling, casts his eyes upon the ground. But raises them suddenly on hearing his own name.)*

CRATCHIT. *(raising his glass)* Mr. Scrooge! I give you Mr. Scrooge, the Founder of the Feast!

MRS CRATCHIT. *(reddening angrily)* The Founder of the Feast indeed! I wish I had him here. I'd give him a piece of my mind to feast upon, and I hope he'd have a good appetite for it!

CRATCHIT. *(placating her)* My dear, the children, Christmas Day.

MRS CRATCHIT. It should be Christmas Day, I am sure, on which one drinks the health of such an odious, stingy, hard, unfeeling man as Mr. Scrooge. You know he is, Robert! Nobody knows it better than you do, poor fellow.

CRATCHIT. *(mildly)* My dear, Christmas Day.

MRS CRATCHIT. I'll drink his health for your sake and the Day's – not for his. Long life to him! A merry Christmas and a happy New Year! He'll be very merry and very happy. I have no doubt!

(All the children glumly drink the toast. Then after a long, somber silence, they become merrier than ever.)

CRATCHIT. You know, Master Peter, I have my eye on a situation for you that would bring in full five and sixpence weekly.

MARTHA. All week long we've been attaching holly to bonnets at the milliner's. Why on Christmas week we work twelve hours a day! But tomorrow I shall lie abed all morning. After all, it is a holiday. Last week I saw a countess and lord at the shop. Imagine, a real countess and lord! The lord wasn't any taller than Peter!

(All laugh. TINY TIM sings a song about a little child lost in the snow. It begins to get dark and snow falls pretty heavily. People scurry about the street laden with gifts.)

SCROOGE. Where are all these people rushing to?

CHRISTMAS PRESENT. Visiting their families and friends.

SCROOGE. Judging by the number of them on their way you'd think there'd be no one at home to give them welcome!

(As the people pass the ghost waves his hand over them and they get the Christmas Spirit and become merry. **THE LAMPLIGHTER** *sternly dressing the street with specks of light laughs out loudly as the spirit pours out from his generous hand its bright and harmless mirth.)*

CHRISTMAS PRESENT. Little does the lamplighter know that he has company at Christmas!

(Suddenly without any warning they find themselves in a desolate place.)

SCROOGE. What place is this?

CHRISTMAS PRESENT. A place where miners live who labor in the bowels of the earth. But they know me, see!

(A **MINER'S FAMILY** *sits about a fire singing a Christmas song. An old man leads them.)*

Hold onto my robe!

SCROOGE. Where are we going? Not to sea?

CHRISTMAS PRESENT. To sea. Look there!

SCROOGE. A light.

CHRISTMAS PRESENT. A lighthouse. Even there two men who watch the light have made a fire and join their horny hands across the table and wish each other Merry Christmas in their can of grog. Even they, their faces damaged and scarred with hard weather, strike up a sturdy song that is like the gale itself. And there beyond any shore, a lonely ship on the black and heaving sea, through lonely darkness, over an unknown abyss, whose depths are secrets as profound as death, sailors hum a Christmas tune or have a Christmas thought or speak below their breath to their companion of some bygone Christmas Day, with homeward hopes belonging to it.

(Suddenly, to **SCROOGE***'s surprise in the moaning of the wind he hears his nephew's laugh. They find themselves in a bright dry gleaming room. [A Punch and Judy stage, with Scrooge's* **NEPHEW** *as the puppeteer. Puppets of Punch, disguised as Scrooge, and a Ghost.])*

GHOST. Woooo!

PUNCH. *(turns toward ghost)*

GHOST. *(disappears)*

PUNCH. *(turns away)*

GHOST. Woooo!

PUNCH. *(turns toward ghost)*

GHOST. *(disappears)*

PUNCH. *(turns away)*

GHOST. Woooo!

PUNCH. *(turns toward ghost)*

GHOST. *(disappears)*

PUNCH. *(Sees ghost. Screams, faints)*

NEPHEW. Ha, ha! Ha, ha, ha! *(holding his sides rolling his head and twisting his face into the most extravagant contortions)*

(Scrooge's **NIECE** *by marriage and all their circle of friends join in.)*

NEPHEW. He said that Christmas was a humbug as I live! He believed it, too!

NIECE. More shame for him, Fred!

NEPHEW. He's a comical old fellow, that's the truth, and not so pleasant as he might be. However, his offenses carry their own punishment, and I have nothing to say against him.

NIECE. I'm sure he is very rich, Fred. At least you always told me so.

NEPHEW. What of that, my dear? His wealth is of no use to him. He don't do any good with it. He don't make himself comfortable with it. He hasn't the satisfaction of thinking – ha, ha, ha! – that he is ever going to benefit us with it.

NIECE. I have no patience with him!

(The others all agree.)

NEPHEW. Oh, I have! I am sorry for him, I couldn't be angry with him if I tried. Who suffers by his ill whims? Himself, always. Here, he takes into his head to dislike us, and he won't come and dine with us. What's the consequence? He don't lose much of a dinner –

NIECE. *(interrupting)* Indeed, I think he loses a very good dinner.

(All agree.)

NEPHEW. Well! I am very glad to hear it because I haven't any great faith in these young housekeepers. What do *you* say, Topper?

TOPPER. We bachelors are wretched outcasts. *(eyeing a plump young beauty)* But I have no right to express an opinion on the subject.

NIECE. *(clapping her hands)* Do go on, Fred! He never finishes what he begins to say! He is such a ridiculous fellow!

NEPHEW. *(laughing his infectious laugh)* I was only going to say that the consequences of his taking a dislike to us, and not making merry with us, is, as I think, that he loses some pleasant moments, which could do him no harm. I am sure he loses pleasanter companions than he can find in his own thoughts either in his moldy old office, or his dusty chambers. I mean to give him the same chance every year, whether he likes it or not, for I pity him. He may rail at Christmas till he dies, but he can't help thinking better of it – I defy him – if he finds me going there, in good temper, year after year, and saying, Uncle Scrooge, how are you? If it only puts him in the vein to leave his poor clerk fifty pounds, *that's* something, and I think I shook him yesterday.

*(All laugh. They play blindman's bluff. **TOPPER**, though blindfolded, relentlessly pursues the **PLUMP BEAUTY**.)*

PLUMP BEAUTY. It isn't fair! Why I no more believe that you are blind than I believe you have eyes in your boots!

TOPPER. *(catching her)* The hair is familiar. Who can it be? Let me touch your headdress. I'm sorry but I'm stumped. I don't know you at all.

PLUMP BEAUTY. Oh pooh!

TOPPER. Perhaps if this ring fits, then I'd know you *(slipping a ring on her finger)* Then I'd know you anywhere.

NEPHEW. Let's play "Yes and No"!

CHRISTMAS PRESENT. It's growing late.

SCROOGE. Spirit, couldn't we stay until the guests leave?

CHRISTMAS PRESENT. This cannot be done.

SCROOGE. Here's a new game. One half hour, Spirit, only one!

NEPHEW. Now here's how you play "Yes and No." I will think of something and the rest of you must find out what, but I can only answer your questions yes or no, as is the case.

ALL THE GUESTS. *(asking in turn)* Is it an animal?

NEPHEW. *(laughing at each response)* Yes!

GUEST. Is it a live animal?

NEPHEW. Yes!

GUEST. Is it a disagreeable animal?

NEPHEW. Yes!

GUEST. Is it a savage animal?

NEPHEW. Yes!

GUEST. Does it growl and grunt sometimes?

NEPHEW. Yes.

GUEST. Can it talk?

NEPHEW. Yes.

GUEST. Does it live in London?

NEPHEW. Yes.

GUEST. Does it walk about the streets?

NEPHEW. Yes.

GUEST. Does it perform in a show?

NEPHEW. No.

GUEST. Is it led about?

NEPHEW. No.

GUEST. Does it live in a menagerie?

NEPHEW. No.

GUEST. Is it killed in a market?

NEPHEW. No.

GUEST. Is it a horse?

NEPHEW. No.

GUEST. Is it an ass?

NEPHEW. *(tempted to say yes)* No.

GUEST. Is it a cow?

NEPHEW. No.

GUEST. Is it a bull?

NEPHEW. No.

GUEST. Is it a tiger?

NEPHEW. No.

GUEST. A pig?

NEPHEW. No.

GUEST. A cat?

NEPHEW. No.

GUEST. Is it a bear?

NEPHEW. No.

PLUMP BEAUTY. I have found it out! I know what it is, Fred! I know what it is!

NEPHEW. What is it?

PLUMP BEAUTY. It's your Uncle Scro-o-o-oge!

NEPHEW. It certainly is!

TOPPER. Not fair. When we asked if it was a bear you should have said yes. You were trying to throw us off the track.

NEPHEW. He has given us plenty of merriment, I am sure, and it would be ungrateful not to drink his health. Here is a glass of mulled wine ready to our hand at the moment, and I say, "Uncle Scrooge!"

ALL. *(raising their glasses)* Well! Uncle Scrooge.

NEPHEW. A Merry Christmas and a Happy New Year to the old man, whatever he is! He wouldn't take it from me, but may he have it nonetheless. Uncle Scrooge!

(**SCROOGE** *has become visibly light of heart and almost toasts the company in return. The scene before them vanishes and* **SCROOGE** *and the* **SPIRIT** *are again upon their travels. The spirit has aged visibly.*)

SCROOGE. This has been a long night, if it is only a night. Your hair's turned gray. Are spirits' lives so short?

CHRISTMAS PRESENT. My life upon this globe is very brief. It ends tonight.

SCROOGE. *(cries out in amazement)* Tonight?

CHRISTMAS PRESENT. Tonight at midnight. Hark! The time is drawing near.

(The chimes are heard ringing three-quarters past eleven.)

SCROOGE. Forgive me if I am not justified in what I ask. But I see something strange, and not belonging to yourself, protruding from your skirts. Is it a foot or a claw?

CHRISTMAS PRESENT. *(sadly)* It may be a claw for the flesh there is upon it. Look here.

(The spirit opens its robe and discloses two children, a boy and a girl, yellow, meager, ragged, scowling, wolfish, stale, and shriveled as if pinched and twisted by age – monsters of horror and dread.)

SCROOGE. *(Starting back, appalled. He tries to say something good about them.)* Why they are…they are… *(chokes)* Spirit, are they yours?

CHRISTMAS PRESENT. *(looking down upon them)* They are Man's, and they cling to me, appealing from their fathers. This boy is Ignorance. This girl is Want. Beware them both, and all of their degree, but most of all beware this boy for on his brow I see that written which is Doom, unless the writing be erased. *(crying out vehemently)* Deny it! *(stretching out his hand toward the city)* Slander those who tell it ye! Admit it for your factious purposes, and make it worse! And bide the end!

SCROOGE. Have they no refuge or resource?

CHRISTMAS PRESENT. Are there no prisons? Are there no workhouses?

(The bell strikes twelve. The spirit vanishes. A phantom draped and hooded approaches **SCROOGE** *gravely, silently, with outstretched hand, like a mist along the ground.)*

SCROOGE. *(bending down upon his knee)* I am in the presence of the ghost of Christmas yet to come?

(The **SPIRIT** *does not answer but points downward with its hand.)*

You are about to show me shadows of the things that have not happened, but will happen in the time before us, is that so, Spirit?

(The **SPIRIT** *whose face is not visible bows its hooded head. Thrilled with a vague uncertain horror)*

Ghost of the future! I fear you more than any specter I have seen. But as I know your purpose is to do me good, and as I hope to be another man from what I was, I am prepared to bear you company, and do it with a thankful heart. Will you not speak to me?

(The **SPIRIT** *points its hand straight before them.)*

Lead on! Lead on! The night is waning fast, and it is precious time to me, I know. Lead on, Spirit!

(The phantom moves away and as it does the city appears about them. They find themselves in the heart of the business district. There the phantom points to a little knot of **BUSINESSMEN**. **SCROOGE** *advances and listens to them talk.)*

FIRST BUSINESSMAN. No, I don't know much about it either way. I only know he's dead.

SECOND BUSINESSMAN. When did he die?

FIRST BUSINESSMAN. Last night, I believe.

THIRD BUSINESSMAN. Why, what was the matter with him? *(takes snuff)* I thought he'd never die.

FIRST BUSINESSMAN. God knows.

SECOND BUSINESSMAN. What has he done with his money?

FIRST BUSINESSMAN. *(yawns)* I haven't heard. Left it to his company, perhaps. He hasn't left it to *me*. That's all I know.

(All three laugh.)

It's likely to be a very cheap funeral, for upon my life I don't know of anybody to go to it. Suppose we make up a party and volunteer?

SECOND BUSINESSMAN. I don't mind going if a lunch is provided. But I must be fed if I make one.

FIRST BUSINESSMAN. Well, I am the most disinterested among you after all, for I would never wear those black gloves they give you as a memento and I never eat lunch. But I'll offer to go if anybody else will. When I come to think of it, I'm not at all sure that I wasn't his most particular friend, for we used to stop and speak whenever we met. Bye-bye!

*(They all stroll off in different directions. **SCROOGE** looks to the phantom for an explanation but it only glides on down the street and points to two other **BUSINESSMEN**.)*

MAN A. How are you?

MAN B. How are you?

MAN A. Well! Old Scratch has got his own at last, hey?

MAN B. So I am told. Cold isn't it?

MAN A. Seasonable for Christmastime. You're not a skater, I suppose?

MAN B. No. No. Something else to think of. Good morning!

*(They part. The phantom now leads **SCROOGE** to a den in the wretched part of town whose whole quarter reeks with crime, with filth, with misery. Two women like shopping bag ladies and a vulture-like man enter a junk man's shop.)*

BAG LADY. Let the charwoman alone to be the first! Let the laundress alone to be the second, and let the undertaker's man alone to be the third. Look here, Old Joe, here's a chance! If we haven't all three met here without meaning it!

OLD JOE. *(removing his pipe from his mouth)* You couldn't have met in a better place. Come into the parlor. You were made free of it long ago, you know, and the other two an't strangers. Stop till I shut the door of the shop. Ah! How it shrieks! There an't such a rusty bit of metal in the place as its own hinges, I believe, and I'm sure there's no such old bones here as mine. Ha, ha! We're all suitable to our calling, we're well matched. Come into the parlor. Come into the parlor.

(The parlor is behind a curtain of rags.)

BAG LADY. *(throws her bundle on the floor and sits down in a flaunting manner on a stool, crossing her elbows on her knees, and looking with a bold defiance at the other two)* What odds, then! What odds, Mrs. Dilber? Every person has a right to take care of themselves. *He* always did!

MRS DILBER. *(a laundress)* That's true, indeed! No man more so.

BAG LADY. Why, then, don't stand staring as if you was afraid, woman, who's the wiser? We're not going to pick holes in each other's coats, I suppose?

OLD JOE & MRS DILBER No, indeed! We should hope not.

BAG LADY. Very well, then! That's enough. Who's the worse for the loss of a few things like these? Not a dead man, I suppose.

MRS DILBER. *(laughing)* No, indeed.

BAG LADY. If he wanted to keep 'em after he was dead, a wicked old screw, why wasn't he natural in his lifetime? If he had been he'd have had somebody to look after him when he was struck by death, instead of lying gasping out his last there, alone by himself.

MRS DILBER. It's the truest word that ever was spoke. It's a judgment on him.

BAG LADY. I wish it was a little heavier one. And it should have been, you may depend upon it, if I could have laid my hands on anything else. Open that bundle, Old Joe, and let me know the value of it. Speak out plain. I'm not afraid to be the first, nor afraid for them to see it. We knew pretty well that we were helping ourselves, before we met here, I believe. It's no sin. Open the bundle, Joe.

MRS DILBER. Me first. *(She opens her bundle.)*

OLD JOE. *(jotting down the sum)* A seal, a pencil case, a pair of sleeve buttons, a brooch of no great value. Sheets and towels, a little wearing apparel, two old-fashioned silver teaspoons, a pair of sugar tongs, and a few boots. *(Writes an amount on the wall.)* That's your account and I wouldn't give another six-pence if I was to be boiled for not doing it. I always give too much to ladies. It's a weakness of mine, and that's the way I ruin myself. That's your account. If you asked me for another penny and made it an open question, I'd repent for being so liberal, and knock off half a crown.

BAG LADY. And now undo *my* bundle, Joe.

OLD JOE. *(undoes a great many knots and drags out some stuff)* What do you call this? Bed curtains!

BAG LADY. *(leaning forward on her crossed arms)* Ah! Bed curtains!

OLD JOE. You don't mean to say you took 'em down, rings and all, with him lying there?

BAG LADY. Yes I do. Why not?

OLD JOE. You were born to make your fortune and you'll certainly do it.

BAG LADY. *(coolly)* I certainly shan't hold my hand, when I can get anything in it by reaching it out, for the sake of such a man as he was, I promise you, Joe. Don't drop that oil upon the blankets, now.

OLD JOE. His blankets?

BAG LADY. Whose else's do you think? He isn't likely to take cold without 'em, I dare say.

OLD JOE. *(stopping and looking up)* I hope he didn't die of anything catching? Eh?

BAG LADY. Don't you be afraid of that. I an't so fond of his company that I'd loiter about him for such things, if he did. Ah! You may look through that shirt till your eyes ache, but you won't find a hole in it, nor a threadbare place. It's the best he had and a fine one too. They'd have wasted it, if it hadn't been for me.

OLD JOE. What do you call wasting of it?

BAG LADY. Putting it on him to be buried in to be sure. *(with a laugh)* Some-body was fool enough to do it, but I took it off again. If calico an't good enough for such a purpose, it isn't good enough for anything. It's quite as becoming to the body. He can't look uglier than he did in that one.

(**OLD JOE** *writes her sum on the wall, then hands her money.*)

Ha, ha! This is the end of it, you see! He frightened everyone away from him when he was alive, to profit us when he was dead! Ha, ha, ha!

SCROOGE. *(shuddering from head to foot)* Spirit! I see, I see. The case of this unhappy man might be my own. My life tends that way, now. Merciful Heaven, what is this!

(**SCROOGE** *recoils in terror for the scene has changed. Before him on a bare uncurtained bed beneath a ragged sheet, lies a still form.* **SCROOGE** *looks toward the phantom who points to the head of the body.*)

Oh cold, cold, rigid, dreadful Death, set up thine altar here, and dress it with such terrors as thou hast at thy command for this is thy dominion! But of the loved, revered, and honored head, thou canst not turn one hair to thy dread purposes, or make one feature odious. It is not that the hand is heavy and will fall down when released, it is not that the heart and pulse are still, but that the hand was open, generous, and true, the heart brave, warm, and tender, and the pulse a man's. Strike, Shadow, strike! And see his good deeds springing from the wound, to sow the world with life immortal! Spirit! This is a fearful place. In leaving it, I shall not leave its lesson, trust me. Let us go!

(The ghost points an unmoving finger to the corpse's head.)

SCROOGE. *(cont.)* I understand you, and I would do it, if I could. But I have not the power, Spirit. I have not the power. If there is any person in this town who feels emotion caused by this man's death, show that person to me, Spirit, I beseech you!

(The phantom spreads its dark robe before him for a moment, like a wing and withdrawing it, reveals a room by daylight, where a mother and her children are. There is a knock at the door – her husband eneters, a man whose face is careworn and depressed, though he is young.)

SHE. Is there any news? *(pause)* Tell me is it good or bad?

HE. Bad.

SHE. We are quite ruined?

HE. No. There is hope yet, Caroline.

SHE. If *he* relents, there is! Nothing is past hope, if such a miracle has happened.

HE. He is past relenting. He is dead.

SHE. *(with a gentle heartfelt sincerity)* Oh thank God. *(clasping her hands)* What am I saying? God forgive me.

HE. What the half-drunken woman, whom I told you of last night, said to me when I tried to see him and obtain a week's delay, and what I thought was a mere excuse to avoid me, turns out to have been quite true. He was not only very ill, but dying, then.

SHE. To whom will our debt be transferred?

HE. I don't know. But before that time we shall be ready with the money, and even though we were not, it would be bad fortune indeed to find so merciless a creditor in his successor. We may sleep tonight with light hearts, Caroline.

(They embrace. The children cluster about them.)

SCROOGE. Let me see some tenderness connected with a death, or that dark chamber, Spirit, which we left just now, will be forever present to me.

(They enter Bob Cratchit's house. The mother and the children are seated round the fire still as statues.)

PETER. *(reading from a book)* "And he took a child, and set him in the midst of them."

MRS CRATCHIT. *(lays her sewing upon the table and puts her hand up to her face)* The color hurts my eyes.

SCROOGE. The color? Ah, poor Tiny Tim!

MRS CRATCHIT. They're better now again. It makes them weak by candlelight, and I wouldn't show weak eyes to your father when he comes home, for the world. It must be near his time.

PETER. *(shutting his book)* Past it, rather. But I think he's walked a little slower than he used, these few last evenings, Mother.

(long silence among them)

MRS CRATCHIT. I have known him walk with… I have known him walk with Tiny Tim upon his shoulder, very fast indeed.

PETER. *(exclaiming)* And so have I, often.

ANOTHER CHILD. And so have I.

MRS CRATCHIT. But he was very light to carry *(resumes her work)*, and his father loved him so, that it was no trouble – no trouble. And there is your father at the door! *(She rushes to meet him.)*

*(**BOB CRATCHIT** enters. She brings him tea, the children climb upon his lap.)*

CHILD. *(kissing his cheeks)* Don't mind it, Father. Don't be grieved!

CRATCHIT. I'm not. I'm not. Ah, it's good to be here with you all. The needle-work is progressing nicely. It should be done by Sunday.

MRS CRATCHIT. Sunday! You went today, then, Robert?

CRATCHIT. Yes, my dear. I wish you could have gone. It would have done you good to see how green a place it is. But you'll see it often. I promised him that I would walk there on a Sunday. *(breaking down and crying)* My little child! My little child!

(Rises and leaves room and enters room where **TINY TIM** *lies surrounded by candles and Christmas things.* **CRATCHIT** *kisses the little face. Reenters room.)*

CRATCHIT. *(cont.)* I met Mr. Scrooge's nephew today in the street. I have scarcely seen him before but once and on seeing me he said I looked "just a little down, you know." On which, because he is the pleasantest-spoken gentleman you ever heard, I told him. And he said, "I am heartily sorry for it, Mr. Cratchit, and heartily sorry for your good wife." Bye the bye, how he ever knew *that*, I don't know.

MRS CRATCHIT. Knew what, my dear?

CRATCHIT. Why, that you were a good wife.

PETER. Everybody knows that!

CRATCHIT. Well observed, my boy! I hope they do. "Heartily sorry," he said, "for your good wife. If I can be of service to you in any way," he said, "this is where I live – pray come to me," and gave me his card! Now, it wasn't for the sake of anything he might be able to do for us, so much as for his kind way, that this was quite delightful. It really seemed as if he had known our Tiny Tim, and felt with us.

MRS CRATCHIT. I'm sure he's a good soul.

CRATCHIT. You would be surer of it, my dear, if you saw and spoke to him. I shouldn't be at all surprised, mark what I say, if he got Peter a better situation.

MRS CRATCHIT. Only hear that, Peter.

ONE OF THE GIRLS. And then Peter will be keeping company with someone and setting up for himself.

PETER *(grinning)* Get along with you!

CRATCHIT. It's just as likely as not one of these days, though there's plenty of time for that, my dears. But however and whenever we part from one another I am sure we shall none of us forget poor Tiny Tim – shall we – or this first parting that there was among us?

ALL. Never, Father!

CRATCHIT. And I know, I know, my dears, that when we recollect how patient and how mild he was, although he was a little, little child, we shall not quarrel easily among ourselves, and forget poor Tiny Tim in doing it.

ALL. No, never, Father!

(**MRS CRATCHIT** *kisses him. His daughters kiss him. He and* **PETER** *shake hands.*)

CRATCHIT. Spirit of Tiny Tim, thy childish essence was from God. And let us always think of Tiny Tim at Christmas – Christmas whose mighty founder was a child himself. I am very happy! I am very happy!

SCROOGE. Specter, something informs me that our parting moment is at hand. I know it. But I know not how. Tell me what man that was whom we saw lying dead?

(*The* **SPIRIT** *points.*)

This court through which we hurry now is where my place of occupation is, and has been for a length of time. I see the house. Let me behold what I shall be in days to come.

(*The spirit points in the opposite direction.*)

The house is yonder. Why do you point away?

(*They pass through an iron gate into a churchyard. The spirit stands among the graves and points to a single stone.*)

Before I draw nearer to that stone to which you point, answer me one question. Are these the shadows of the things that Will be, or are they shadows of the things that May be, only?

(*The ghost points down to the grave.*)

Men's courses will foreshadow certain ends, to which, if persevered in, they must lead. But if the courses be departed from, the ends will change. Say it is thus with what you show me.

(The spirit does not move. Creeping toward the spirit and following the finger, reads upon the stone of the neglected grave his own name: Ebenezer Scrooge. Then falling to his knees)

SCROOGE. *(cont.)* Am *I* that man who lay upon the bed?

(The finger points from the grave to him and back again.)

No, Spirit! Oh no, no! Spirit *(clutching at its robe)* hear me! I am not the man I was. I will not be the man I must have been but for this intercourse. Why show me this if I am past all hope?

*(The **SPIRIT**'s hand appears to shake. Falling on the ground before it)*

Good Spirit, your nature intercedes for me and pities me. Assure me that I yet may change these shadows you have shown me, by an altered life!

*(The **SPIRIT**'s hand trembles.)*

I will honor Christmas in my heart, and try to keep it all the year. I will live in the Past, the Present, and the Future. The spirits of all three will strive within me. I will not shut out the lessons that they teach. Oh, tell me I may sponge away the writing on this stone!

*(**SCROOGE** catches the spectral hand in his agony. It tries to free itself. He detains it. It repulses him. Then holding up his hands in on last prayer to have his fate reversed, the **SPIRIT** alters, shrinks, and collapses into a bedpost.)*

Scene Five
The Next Morning

SCROOGE. I will live in the Past, the Present, and the Future! *(scrambling out of bed)* The spirits of all three shall strive within me. Oh, Jacob Marley! Heaven and the Christmas Time be praised for this! I say it on my knees, old Jacob, on my knees!

(His face is wet with tears, his voice broken from sobbing violently. He examines the bed curtains.)

The bed curtains are not torn down. *(folding bed curtains in his arms)* They are not torn down rings and all. They are here. I am here, the shadows of the things that would have been may be dispelled. They will be. I know they will!

(His hands have been busy with his garments all this time turning them inside out, putting them on upside down, tearing them, mislaying them, making them parties to every kind of extravagance. Laughing and crying in the same breath)

I don't know what to do! I am as light as a feather, I am as happy as an angel, I am as merry as a schoolboy, I am as giddy as a drunken man. A Merry Christmas to everybody! A Happy New Year to all the world! Hallo here! Whoop! Hallo! *(turning in circles, looking about the room)* There's the saucepan that the gruel was in! There's the door by which the ghost of Jacob Marley entered! There's the corner where the ghost of Christmas Present sat! There's the window where I saw the wandering Spirits! It's all right, it's all true, it all happened. Ha, ha, ha! *(lets out a splendid laugh)* I don't know what day of the month it is! I don't know how long I've been among the Spirits. I don't know anything, I'm quite a baby. Never mind. I don't care. I'd rather be a baby. Hallo! Whoop! Hallo here! *(The church bells ring out lusty peals.)* Church bells, oh glorious, glorious – Ding, dong! *(opens window and puts out his head)* No fog, no mist, clear, bright, jovial, stirring, cold, cold, piping for the blood to dance to, golden sunlight, heavenly sky, sweet fresh air, merry bells. Oh, glorious. Glorious!

(calling to a **BOY** *in Sunday clothes)*

What's today?

BOY. Eh?

SCROOGE. What's today, my fine fellow?

BOY. Today – why, Christmas Day.

SCROOGE. *(to himself)* It's Christmas Day! I haven't missed it. The Spirits have done it all in one night. They can do anything they like. Of course they can. Of course they can. Hallo, my fine fellow.

BOY. Hallo!

SCROOGE. Do you know the poulterer's in the next street but one, at the corner?

BOY. I should hope I did.

SCROOGE. An intelligent boy. A remarkable boy! Do you know whether they've sold the prize turkey that was hanging up there? Not the little prize turkey, the big one?

BOY. What, the one as big as me?

SCROOGE. What a delightful boy! It's a pleasure to talk to him. Yes, my buck.

BOY. It's hanging there now.

SCROOGE. Is it? Go and buy it.

BOY. *(thumbs his nose)* Take a walk!

SCROOGE. No, no. I am in earnest. Go and buy it, and tell 'em to bring it here, that I may give them the direction where to take it. Come back with the man and I'll give you a shilling. Come back with him in less than five minutes and I'll give you half a crown.

(The **BOY** *is off like a shot. Whispering)*

I'll send it to Bob Cratchit's. *(rubs his hands and spits with a laugh.)* He shan't know who sends it. It's twice the size of Tiny Tim. Joe Miller never made such a joke as sending it to Bob's will be!

(Writes a note with an unsteady hand. Then while waiting for the poulterer's man, the door knocker catches his eye.)

SCROOGE. *(cont.)* What a wonderful knocker! What an honest expression it has in its face! I scarcely ever looked at it before. I shall love it as long as I live! Here's the turkey. Hallo! Whoop! How are you! Merry Christmas!

(They **BOY** *reenters carrying a young turkey as large as himself. A man accompanies him)*

That *is* a turkey! He could never have stood upon his legs, that bird. He would have snapped 'em short off in a minute, like sticks of sealing wax. Why, it's impossible to carry that to Camden Town. You must have a cab.

(Chuckling all the while he pays for the turkey, pays for the cab and recompenses the **BOY***. Then he sits down in his chair and chuckles till he cries. Then he shaves while dancing and dresses himself and goes out in the street, beaming at everyone as he walks along with his hands behind his back.)*

SEVERAL PASSERS-BY. Good morning, sir! A Merry Christmas to you!

SCROOGE. Of all the blithe sounds I have ever heard those were the blithest in my ears.

(The two **GENTLEMEN** *from the charities approach. Quickening his pace and taking the old* **GENTLEMAN** *by both hands.)*

My dear sir, how do you do? I hope you succeeded yesterday. It was very kind of you. A Merry Christmas to you, sir!

GENTLEMAN. Mr. Scrooge?

SCROOGE. Yes, that is my name, and I fear it may not be pleasant to you. Allow me to ask your pardon. And will you have the goodness... *(whispers in his ear)*

GENTLEMAN. *(as if his breath were gone)* Lord bless me! My dear Mr. Scrooge, are you serious?

SCROOGE. If you please, not a farthing less. A great many back payments are included in it, I assure you. Will you do me that favor?

GENTLEMAN. *(shaking hands with him)* My dear sir, I don't know what to say to such munifi–

SCROOGE. Don't say anything, please. Come and see me. Will you come and see me?

GENTLEMAN. *(clearly meaning it)* I will!

SCROOGE. Thank'ee, I am much obliged to you. I thank you fifty times. Bless you!

(walks on patting children on the head until he arrives at his nephew's house and knocks at the door)

Is your master at home, my dear? Nice girl. Very.

GIRL. Yes, sir.

SCROOGE. Where is he, my love?

GIRL. He's in the dining room, sir, along with mistress. I'll show you upstairs, if you please.

SCROOGE. Thank'ee. He knows me. I'll go in here, my dear.

*(poking in his head as **NEPHEW** and **GUESTS** are toasting him)*

Fred!

NIECE. *(terribly startled, lets out a little shriek)*

NEPHEW. Why bless my soul! Who's that?

SCROOGE. It's I. Your Uncle Scrooge. I have come to dinner. Will you let me in, Fred?

*(**FRED** practically shakes his arm off. Stunned expression on the face of all the company. Blackout.)*

Scene Six
Scrooge and Marley's. The next morning.

SCROOGE. If only I can catch Bob Cratchit coming late! That's the thing I have set my heart upon. Nine o'clock. No Bob. A quarter past. No Bob. He's a full eighteen and a half behind his time.

(**CRATCHIT** *hurries in with his hat and muffler already off and takes his place on his stool in a jiffy and drives away with his pen as if he were trying to overtake nine o'clock. Growls.*)

Hallo! What do you mean by coming here at this time of day?

CRATCHIT. I am very sorry, sir. I *am* behind my time.

SCROOGE. You are? Yes, I think you are. Step this way, if you please.

CRATCHIT. *(pleading)* It's only once a year, sir. It shall not be repeated. I was making rather merry yesterday, sir.

SCROOGE. You were? Yes, I believe you were. Now, I'll tell you what, my friend. I am not going to stand this sort of thing any longer. And therefore

(*leaping from his stool and giving* **BOB** *such a dig in the waistcoat that he staggers back*)

…and therefore, I am about to raise your salary!

CRATCHIT. *(threatening* **SCROOGE** *with a ruler)* Don't take another step near me or I'll knock you out and call the people in the court to help and bring a straight waistcoat.

SCROOGE. A Merry Christmas Bob! *(clapping him on the back)* A Merrier Christmas, Bob, my good fellow, than I have given you for many a year! I'll raise your salary, and endeavor to assist your struggling family, and we will discuss your affairs this very afternoon over a Christmas bowl of smoking bishop, Bob! If there be room for two I'd like to be a second father to that boy of yours, Tiny Tim. Make up the fires and buy another coal scuttle before you dot another "i", Bob Cratchit!

CRATCHIT. Mr. Scrooge, may I stand you to a drink?

SCROOGE. No, I plan to live as an abstainer and have no further need of spirits. *(laughs outrageously at his own joke)* And so, as Tiny Tim observed...

TINY TIM. *(throwing away his crutch and leaping onto* **SCROOGE**'s *shoulder)* God bless us every one!

Also by
Charles Ludlam...

The Artificial Jungle
Big Hotel
Bluebeard
Caprice
Camille
Conquest of the Universe or When Queens Collide
Corn
Der Ring Gott Farblonjet
The Enchanted Pig
Eunuchs of the Forbidden City
Exquisite Torture
Galas
The Grand Tarot
Hot Ice
How to Write a Play
Isle of the Hermaphrodites or the Murdered Minion
Jack and the Beanstalk
Le Bourgeois Avent-Garde
Love's Tangled Web
Medea
The Mystery of Irma Vep - A Penny Dreadful
Reverse Psychology
Salammbo
Secret Lives of the Sexists
Stage Blood
Turds in Hell
Utopia Incorporated
The Ventriloquist's Wife

Please visit our website **samuelfrench.com** for complete
descriptions and licensing information.

OTHER TITLES AVAILABLE FROM SAMUEL FRENCH

THE MYSTERY OF IRMA VEP
- A PENNY DREADFUL

Charles Ludlam

Comedy / 2m, playing various roles / Simple Sets

This definitive spoof of Gothic melodramas, recently revived Off-Broadway to raves, is a quick change marathon in which two actors play all the roles. A sympathetic werewolf, a vampire and an Egyptian princess brought to life when her tomb is opened make this a comedy that has everything.

"Far and away the funniest two hours on a New York stage...What more meaningful gift could Ludlam bequeath [audiences] than to leave them eternally laughing."
– *The New York Times*

"A really good laugh...The story has to be seen to be believed."
– *The New York Post*

"Lunatic fun that keeps you in stitches."
– *The New York Daily News*

"A true vaudeville tour de farce...It's wonderful."
– *Time*

"A hearty mixture of thrills, laughter and extravagant showmanship."
– *The Village Voice*

OTHER TITLES AVAILABLE FROM SAMUEL FRENCH

CAPRICE

Charles Ludlam

Comedy / 6m, 5f, extras, double casting and cross-gender casting possible / Various Interiors

The comical and tragical history of Claude Caprice, tastemaker and couturier, from the master of the Ridiculous!

Caprice introduces Babushka, the world's first live fashion model, the bra-called "freedom," the "gownless evening strap," and the ultimate fashion statement – sackcloth and ashes – in his keen competition with arch-rival Twyfibrd Adamant, who uses Tata, a fashion spy, to undermine Caprice and his lover Adrian. Baroness Zuni Feinschmecker is a slave of fashion, and her husband Harry discovers the world of fashion – and a new sexual identity – in the House of Caprice.

Caprice is a comic delight, containing a uniquely unapologetic presentation of overtly homosexual characters. The Ballet du Macquillage – a dance for lipstick, powder, rouge, and mascara – is not to be missed.

OTHER TITLES AVAILABLE FROM SAMUEL FRENCH

CONQUEST OF THE UNIVERSE
OR
WHEN QUEENS COLLIDE

Charles Ludlam

Comedy / 7m, 8f, extras, double casting and cross-gender casting possible) / Various Settings

Another collage epic by the master of The Ridiculous Theatre, a futuristic tale of war across the universe!

Tamberlaine, President of Earth, proceeds from planet to planet, capturing and enslaving Bajazeth and Zabina – King and Queen of Mars – Venus, and Natolia, Queen of Saturn, among others. Cosroe, a Martian prince and twin brother of Zabina, leads the rebel forces against Tamberlaine in Ludlam's mind-bendingexperimental classic, his theater of "sexual, imperialistic war." Literary, film, and dramatic treasures are ransacked and pillaged for the hilarious dialogue and multiple plots in this unbridled original, humorous tale of unbridaled space queens!

OTHER TITLES AVAILABLE FROM SAMUEL FRENCH

DER RING GOTT FARBLONJET

Charles Ludlam

Comedy / 12m, 17f, double casting and cross-gender casting possible / Various settings

Wagner's entire Ring cycle - *Das Rheingold, Die Walkure, Siegfried*, and *Gotterdammerung* - is compressed and parodied in this three-hour Ridiculous Theatre spectacle. According to Ludlam, "In this work we will launch a complete assault on the use of language in the theater. The dialogue will telescope the past, present, and future history of the English tongue into a new expressive idiom. By cutting across linguistic barriers of the Indo-European group, this 'theatrical esperanto' will eliminate the usual nationalist limitations of spoken drama."

"A comic grand opera...spectacular...heroic."
– *The New York Times*

"A complete myth in full barbaric flower...the work of an artist with a vision."
– *The Village Voice*

"A hilarious, free-wheeling yet faithful reinterpretation of *The Ring*... written in styles ranging from mock-Elizabethan to broken German and Yiddish."
– *SoHo Weekly News*

OTHER TITLES AVAILABLE FROM SAMUEL FRENCH

DEVIL BOYS FROM BEYOND

Buddy Thomas and Kenneth Elliott
Based on an original script by Budy Thomas
Original song, *Sensitive Girl*, music and lyrics
by Drew Fornarola

Comedy / 4m, 4f (all female roles can be played by men in drag) / Unit Set

**Winner! 2009 FringeNYC Overall Excellence Award
for Outstanding Play!
Nominee! 2010 GLAAD Award for Outstanding New York Theater:
Off-Off Broadway!**

Flying Saucers! Backstabbing Bitches! Muscle Hunks and Men in Pumps! Wake up and smell the alien invasion in this outrageous comedy by the author of the off-Broadway hit play, *Crumple Zone*.

"Drag heaven on Earth...*Devil Boys* is a riot."
– *The New York Times*

"Be ready to laugh...a cross-dressing comedy that puts a fresh coat of over-the-top on 1950's sci-fi flicks...Devilishly clever."
– *New York Daily News*

"Two shirtless hunks, four fabulous drag queens, and 90 minutes' worth of high-camp comedy: What more could a fan of ultraridiculous theatrics want? *Devil Boys* is a devilish delight."
– *Back Stage*

"Cheap in all the right ways, the fast, taw dry and very funny *Devil Boys From Beyond* is the Fringe Festival at its best."
– *The New York Post*

SAMUELFRENCH.COM

CPSIA information can be obtained
at www.ICGtesting.com
Printed in the USA
BVHW050645051120
592522BV00004B/391

9 780573 698651